This book belongs to

....

....

This edition first published in 2018 by Alligator Products Ltd
Cupcake is an imprint of Alligator Products Ltd
2nd Floor, 314 Regents Park Road, London N3 2JX

Written by Katherine Sully
Illustrated by Gail Yerril

Copyright © Alligator Products Ltd 2018

All rights reserved.
No part of this publication may be reproduced, stored in a retrieval system, or transmitted in any form or by
any means, electronic, mechanical, photocopying, recording or otherwise, without prior permission.

Printed in China.0686

Lamb says Boo!

cupcake

BAA! MOO! OINK! NEIGH! MAA! What a racket!
It was springtime and was very noisy on the farm.

All the mothers were calling to their new babies.
All the young animals were playing noisy games.

All except for quiet Lamb. She said, "Baa!" in such a little voice that no one noticed her.

One day, Piglet, Goat, Foal and Calf were on their way to the farmyard to play.

"Where are you going?" asked quiet Lamb in her little voice.

But they were making too much noise to hear Lamb. Lamb followed along behind.

Piglet, Goat, Foal and Calf were still making a racket as they passed Goose on their way through the gate. They made such a racket that they woke the little goslings.

Goose was very cross. "Be quiet, you noisy animals!" she honked, pecking at them and flapping her wings.

Piglet, Goat, Foal and Calf ran past Goose.

But quiet Lamb stayed where she was. She was too scared
to run past Goose. Goose glared at her. Lamb decided to go
the long way round to the farmyard on her own.

By the time Lamb trotted into the farmyard, Piglet, Goat, Foal and Calf were deciding what game to play. "Let's play Hide and Seek!" said Piglet, who had the loudest voice.

"Baa," said quiet Lamb in her little voice. "Can I join in?" But no one heard her.

"I'll be the Seeker," said Foal who was the oldest. "You all hide in the farmyard while I count to ten. Then I'll come and find you.

Foal started counting and the animals all ran off to hide. "One, two. . .

Goat hid in the stable where there was a tasty hay net hanging up.

"Three, four. . ."

Piglet ran to the barn and jumped into the straw bales.

"Five, six. . . "

Calf hid behind the henhouse.

"Seven, eight. . . "

And Lamb ran to the dog kennel and hid inside.

"Nine, ten. . . ready or not, here I come!" Foal neighed loudly.

First, Foal found Goat because she was munching so loudly.

Then, she found Piglet who squealed when the straw tickled her.

Next, she found Calf who couldn't help mooing to herself.

But Lamb was so quiet that none of them could find her.
As they passed Lamb's hiding place, she overheard
them talking.

"Lamb is so quiet!" said Calf.

"She wouldn't say *boo* to a goose!" said Goat.

After a while, Lamb couldn't hear any noise
outside the kennel.

She peeped out and looked around. There was no one
there. Piglet, Goat, Foal and Calf had given up looking for
Lamb and had gone home.

Lamb went back to the field alone, the long way round
to avoid Goose.
She thought about what Goat had said.
"Baa," she said quietly. "Boo," she tried instead.

The next morning, Lamb joined Piglet, Goat, Foal and Calf on their way to the farmyard. As usual, they were making a terrible racket.
As usual, Goose was cross when they woke her goslings.

Piglet, Goat, Foal and Calf ran past grumpy Goose.
But Lamb hung back. She took a tiny step towards Goose
and, looking at her feet, she whispered, "Boo."

Goose stopped flapping and honking and
looked at Lamb. "Speak up!" said Goose.
"Baa. . . baa. . . boo?" said Lamb in a wobbly voice.

"Did you say *boo*?" asked Goose, surprised.

"The others said I wouldn't say *boo* to a goose," said Lamb.

Goose honked with laughter.
"That's a way of saying that you are quiet," she told Lamb.

"I just want them to notice me," said Lamb, sadly.

"You need to speak up a little," said Goose.
"And they need to be more quiet."
Then, Goose had an idea.

The next day, Lamb was at the front of the noisy crowd of animals on their way to the farmyard.

When she reached Goose, she stopped and said to the Goose, very quietly so she wouldn't wake the goslings. . ."Boo!"

The other animals stopped and went very quiet.
What will Goose do they wondered? But Goose just smiled
at Lamb and waved her wing. Lamb trotted through the
farmyard gate.

One by one, Piglet, Goat, Foal and Calf
copied Lamb, stopping in front of Goose
and whispering, "Boo!" very quietly.

One by one, Goose
waved them past with a smile.

When they reached the farmyard, Piglet, Goat, Foal and Calf crowded around Lamb.

"I didn't think you'd dare say *boo* to that grumpy goose," said Goat.

"Goose doesn't mind you saying *boo*," explained Lamb, "as long as you say it quietly. Goose is only grumpy when you wake her goslings."

From then on, Lamb played noisy games with Piglet, Goat, Foal and Calf in the farmyard.

But whenever they passed Goose and her goslings, they were all sure to be quiet as a lamb.

The End